THE WIZARD OF OZ

Illustrated by GEORGE C. PEED

*We're on our way, we're on our way
To visit the land of Oz
The most exciting, delighting,
inviting, visit there ever was
'Cause it is, it is, it is, it is the home,
The home of the wonderful Wiz,
the Wiz, the Wiz, the Wiz,
The Wiz, the wonderful
Wizard of Oz.*

Once upon a time, on the great
plains of Kansas, a little girl
named Dorothy lived with her
Aunt Em.

Printed in U.S.A.

One day, as Dorothy was walking home with her little dog, Toto, a huge cyclone came roaring down toward her. "Quick, Toto, into this house,

we'll be safe here."
But, just as she closed the door, the cyclone picked
up the house and sent it spinning through the air,
round and round, higher and higher.

"Oh, I'm getting dizzy. Toto, where are you? Toto! Toto!"

And suddenly she fell down, unconscious.

Hours later, she awakened as the house landed with a bump. She stepped outside, and there stood some strange little people.

"Who are you? And, where am I?"

*We're a happy
bunch of
munchkins
We're here to
welcome you to
the land of Oz,
And why?
Because we like
you, sure do.*

"Oz, I never heard
of it. But, can you
tell me how to get
back to Kansas?
"Only the Wizard
can do that."
"Who?"
"The Wizard,
The Wizard of Oz.
See that yellowbrick
road? Follow it to
Emerald City and
you'll find him
there."
"Oh, thank you.
Come on, Toto."

We're on our way, we're on our way To visit the Wizard of Oz.

A little way down the yellowbrick road, she was startled when a Scarecrow said: "Hello there, who are you?"

"I'm Dorothy, and I'm going to Emerald City to see the Wizard."

"Would you take me with you? Maybe the Wizard will give me a brain instead of straw under my hat."

"I'll be glad to take you. Let's go."

We're on our way, we're on our way
To visit the Wizard of Oz.

Down the yellowbrick road they went, singing happily, when suddenly they heard a strange, creaking noise.

"It's the Tinwoodman."

"Oh, the poor thing, he's all rusty, he needs oil."

She oiled him up and he thanked her. When she told him where she was going, the Tinwoodman said:

"Oh, can I come, too? Maybe the Wizard will give
me a heart."
"Of course, you can, let's go."

On they went, but as they were passing through
the woods, a big lion suddenly jumped out and
roared at them frightening the Tinwoodman, and

the Scarecrow and Toto. This angered Dorothy
and she slapped his face. To their surprise, the
lion started to cry.

"I'm just a cowardly lion, trying to find some courage. I didn't mean any harm."
"Oh, poor lion, come with us, perhaps the Wizard will give you courage.

"Oh, thank you, I will come." At last Dorothy and her friends reached Emerald City and knocked on the door of the wizard's palace.

"Who dares disturb the mighty Wizard?" They were so frightened, they almost ran away, but Dorothy hurriedly explained why they had come. "Then hear this. Destroy my enemy, the Wicked Witch of the West and your wishes shall be granted."

But the Wicked Witch was following their every move in her crystal ball.
"He, he-he, he, destroy me will you."

Summoning her army of Winged Monkeys, she said:

"Bring that Dorothy and her friends here to my castle."

Before they knew what was happening, the Tin-woodman, Scarecrow and Lion found themselves

in the dungeon. Poor Dorothy, ordered to scrub
every floor in the gloomy old castle, thought of
home and began to cry.
"Oooh, Aunt Em, where are you . . . ?"

Somewhere there's sunshine and laughter
Somewhere birds sing all day through
Somewhere, oh, that's where I wish I were
Somewhere out there with you.

This infuriated the Witch. "Stop that sniveling or I'll give you something to really cry about." Suddenly Toto bit her on the leg.

In a rage, the Witch struck Toto. Dorothy became so angry, she threw a bucket of water at her and the Witch screamed:

"Why did you do that? I'm melting away, melting away."
And the Wicked Witch did melt completely away leaving only her Silver Shoes.

Dorothy put on the Silver Shoes, released her friends and they all hurried back to the Wizard. "Your brave actions prove that you, Scarecrow, now have a real brain. And you, Tinwoodman,

have a good heart. And you, Lion, have true courage. As for you, Dorothy, just wish and your Magic
Silver Shoes will take you home."

"Oh, I wish, I wish, and goodbye, dear friends." And soon she was back in Kansas, home again with dear Aunt Em.

And that's the wonderful story of The wonderful Wizard of Oz.